LIBREX-

Also by Marjorie Darke

Emma's Monster

Just Bear and Friends

Written by
MARJORIE DARKE

Illustrated by
DUNCAN SMITH

WALKER BOOKS
AND SUBSIDIARIES
LONDON · BOSTON · SYDNEY

For Sally

First published 1996 by Walker Books Ltd
87 Vauxhall Walk, London SE11 5HJ

This edition published 1997

2 4 6 8 10 9 7 5 3

Text © 1996 Marjorie Darke
Illustrations © 1996 Duncan Smith

The right of Marjorie Darke to be identified as author
of this work has been asserted by her in accordance with the
Copyright, Designs and Patents Act 1988.

This book has been typeset in Plantin Light.

Printed in England by Clays Ltd, St Ives plc

British Library Cataloguing in Publication Data
A catalogue record for this book is
available from the British Library.

ISBN 0-7445-5257-5

CONTENTS

Pip tried the Bear in the shoebox.

JUST BEAR

"Is that yours?" Daniel asked.

Pip nodded. He liked Daniel.

"It's bald." Daniel gave the teddy bear a poke. "And it's got an ear missing. It must be very old."

"Nearly eight," Pip said. "My uncle gave it to me when I was born." This was the first time Daniel had come to Pip's house. He wanted Daniel to be his friend.

"Oh, a *baby* toy," Daniel said, as if that explained how the teddy came to be sitting on the shelf in Pip's bedroom on top of a pile of old comics and next to his muddy football boots. "What do you call him?"

"Just … Bear." Sharing the real name was too risky. Pip thought Daniel might laugh. He laughed a lot.

"Hello, Just Bear!" Nose to nose with the teddy, Daniel burst into a roar of laughter. Taking hold of one leg he swung Just Bear in a circle. Bits of fluff and sawdust began to float towards the carpet.

"Don't!" Pip begged. "The sewing's come undone."

Daniel stopped swinging and took a closer look. Stuffing bulged from a leg and an arm. He pushed his finger through the split in the arm and explored the flatness at the top. "I can feel something."

"Bones?" Pip suggested.

Daniel drew his finger out very quickly. "Toys don't have bones," he said, but he didn't sound too certain. He eyed the teddy. "It might be dead though. It looks dead."

"How do you know?"

Daniel said firmly, "Pickles died last week and he looked just the same."

Remembering that Pickles was Daniel's budgie, Pip found this hard to believe. At the same time he had an uneasy feeling that Daniel must know. He was not at all sure how he felt about having a dead bear sitting on his shelf. "Teddy bears aren't alive, so they can't be dead." He tried to sound as sure as Daniel, but the sad look in the teddy's glass eyes gave him a funny sinking feeling.

"Well, this one must have been, because he's dead now," Daniel insisted.

Pip wanted to ask what would happen next, but Daniel was busy turning Just Bear over and over, squeezing the wobbly leg, prodding the squeak that wouldn't work, flicking the loose eye.

"I've got an idea," he said suddenly.

Pip brightened. He hoped they might be going to buy sweets or an ice lolly, or to kick a football round the park. Or all three, with luck.

"Why don't we have a Funeral?"

"What?" Pip was startled.

"A Funeral. That's what me and Mum did with Pickles. We put him in a shoebox and buried him under the plum tree. So we don't forget where his grave is."

"Oh," Pip said. Then quickly, "All right, let's. Only… "

"Only what?"

"We haven't got a plum tree. We haven't got any trees."

"Doesn't matter. We can write a gravestone instead." Daniel spoke as if he knew everything there was to know about funerals and graves and what you did. "A piece of board'll do. We can write JUST BEAR on it, with the date he died."

"But we don't know when that was."

"Yes, we do. It was today. When his insides fell out. Have you got a shoebox?"

"There's one under my bed." Pip got down on all fours and started to scrabble about. Now there was something practical to do, the funny sinking feeling began to drift away. The more he thought about Daniel's idea the better he liked it. After all, the Bear was *very* old. He had grown out of it long ago. Football was what he liked now. And there was his spaceman set and his electric railway. Bears were for babies.

His hand met something hard. The shoebox! He fished it out and emptied the contents on the floor. Some old-fashioned dinky cars that had belonged to his grandad rolled out, along with a handful of chalks, a broken clockwork mouse, several marbles and an old marmalade sandwich saved from tea three days ago – in case he should feel hungry in the night. The corners had curled and some of the marmalade had stuck to a pink chalk, turning it a dark reddish brown. He tried to lick this clean, but the taste was nasty, so he slipped the chalk into his pocket. Then he blew the dust out of the box. The size looked right. He held it out, but Daniel had pounced on the dinky cars.

"Hey, an old MG! And a steamroller. And a *Bugatti*!" Daniel's eyes grew wide. "Look at *this*!"

Pip looked. The car wasn't anything special. He'd seen it millions of times before. A lot of paint had worn off and one tyre was missing.

"Campbell's Bluebird!" Daniel said in a church voice.

"So?"

"So it used to be the fastest car in the whole world!" Daniel squatted down. "Mind your feet."

Pip hunched on top of his bed and Daniel whooshed Bluebird, then the Bugatti, then the MG underneath. He seemed to have forgotten all about the Funeral.

To hurry things up Pip tried the Bear in the shoebox and found it fitted. He wanted to say so, but Daniel was too busy to listen. Cars shot round the bedroom. Daniel shot after them, making fast racing-car noises.

"Get a move on!" Pip said.

"Wait a minute…"

Pip began to feel cross. The Funeral hadn't been his idea, but he had got used to it. He'd just thought of the perfect place for the grave. At the bottom of the garden, between the cabbages and the compost heap, was a soft patch of soil where he used to make mud pies when he was tiny. He couldn't wait to get digging. "Come *on*!"

"It's raining." Daniel didn't even bother to check.

"No, it isn't. *Let's go now*," and to show he meant it, Pip took the box, got off his bed and started for the stairs.

"Oh, all right!" Daniel parked the cars. "Wait for me…"

It wasn't raining. In fact, it hadn't rained for days and days, and the trowel (Pip's trowel, which Daniel had bagged from the shed) would only go a little way into the ground. The coal shovel that Pip had to use wasn't much better. It was hard work and there was no buried treasure to put in the flowerpot Daniel had brought from the shed, just in case they found any.

They dug.

And dug. But the hole didn't seem to get much bigger. As they went on digging, Pip thought perhaps it would be only fair to let Daniel reach the bottom of the hole first. He took a rest.

"Don't stop. I'll see if this fits." Daniel picked up the box and the lid slipped, showing two furry feet side by side, heels together.

They weren't as worn out as Pip had thought. Lying there, when you couldn't see the bald legs or the flat arm, they looked almost new. He began to dig fast, hoping to unearth a box of gold coins, or a pirate's cutlass, or a space gun. Even an old tennis ball would be better than nothing. Buried treasure was much more exciting than funerals.

He found a worm and two millipedes and an old trouser button, but that was all.

"It's deep enough now." Daniel pushed past him and dropped the box into its hole, scraping at the dug earth which fell with a dull drum sound. He looked up. "Well, aren't you going to help? It's your Bear."

There seemed to be a good deal more soil than they had dug out. They piled it into a mound and used the flowerpot upside down as a gravestone because there wasn't a board. Daniel borrowed the pink chalk and wrote: "JUST BERE" with "DIDE 5 OCTOEBUR" underneath.

Pip added, "love from P. I. PETERS" to stop his bear feeling lonely.

"And D. HIGGS," Daniel wrote.

When they went in for tea it still hadn't rained.

Daniel had gone home and Pip was cleaning his teeth when the first spot hit the bathroom window. A small purr of thunder sounded in the distance. By the time he got into bed, rain was pattering steadily on the glass. The thunder gave a growl.

Pip didn't mind thunder. He waited for it to go away. But there was another growl and then a sparkler of lightning. He counted to find out how many kilometres away the storm was. He didn't mind storms.

"One, two, three, four, five…"

This time the thunder sounded like an angry tiger.

Pip snuggled under the bedclothes and closed his eyes. Usually he went straight to sleep, but tonight this didn't happen. He opened his eyes, then shut them again – and saw a flowerpot. Under the flowerpot was a pile of earth. Under the earth was a box-lid. Under that a bear. A bear who hated thunderstorms.

For a while he tried to count sheep,

making them jump the garden cabbages. But every time they had four feet off the ground they turned into worn bears with one ear missing, frightened glass eyes and stuffing falling out. Bits of fluff blew about in the wind, covering him in a thick fuzzy coat, woolly scarf that pulled up, a furry hat that pulled down. Smothering him.

Growl. *Crackle*. THUMP!

The darkness of the bedroom was lit with sudden sharp spears of silver that poked into every corner, then went out.

Pip sat bolt upright. He couldn't see but he could feel and hear. He felt his front. Oh, relief … pyjamas! Outside thunder went on rolling and bumping round the sky, which was first black, then brilliant with flickerings of silver-blue.

He got out of bed. Crept to the landing, then down the stairs. Noisy music came from the radio in the living-room, so he was able to sneak into the kitchen and open the back door without being heard. The rain had eased off, but a large spot hit his nose as he went out into the garden. Another hit the back of his neck, another fell straight into his mouth. He padded across the wet grass and down the side of the cabbage patch. There were still some chalk letters on the upturned flowerpot. They said:

<pre>
            ERE
  I   R
      o   P.I.P
           D. IGG
</pre>

Pip chucked the flowerpot away and using his hands, scraped and dug till he reached the box. Then he pulled off the lid.

She was still there. A flash of lightning glinted on her glass eyes. They looked bright with hope and very pleased to see him.

"Come on, Brenda," he said kindly, lifting her out. Some of the mud on his hands stuck to her thin fur, but she was quite dry.

Another lightning zigzag tore the sky in half and disappeared behind some houses into the park. Thunder chased it, bellowing like an elephant.

Pip hugged Brenda tight to help her not to be afraid any more. Then he ran. Up the path, across the grass, into the kitchen, up the stairs. No time to wash muddy hands or dry wet feet. Brenda was much too scared.

Pip dived into bed and pulled the bedclothes over them both. It was still warm and very comfortable together. He wondered sleepily what Daniel would say when he saw Brenda back on the shelf. Perhaps he would be too busy racing Bluebird to notice. But if he *wasn't* ... if he *did*...?

Pip yawned and turned over. Somehow it didn't seem to matter.

"Hey, that's mine!"

Football

Pip was kicking a pebble along the pavement. It was a nice pebble, round and greenish with little brown lines like roots on one side. On his back was his haversack. Inside the haversack was his bear, who liked to have a breath of fresh air every now and then. Today was a now-and-then sort of day.

Pip had been to the corner shop with his pocket money and bought some Fizzers. He sucked one as he and the pebble rattled along.

The pebble bumped over the crack between two paving-stones and almost stopped. To help it hurry up, Pip kicked hard.

"Ow!" somebody said.

Wayne, who lived two doors up from Pip, came out of the park gate.

"What did you do that for?" He rubbed his leg.

"Wasn't me," Pip protested. "The pebble did it. Must have bounced off something."

"Me!" Wayne picked up the pebble. Looked at it. Then stuffed it in his pocket.

"Hey, that's mine!" Pip was indignant. Finding that special pebble had taken a long time.

"I'm keeping it safe, that's all," Wayne said loftily. "So it doesn't hit Cassie."

Pip glanced down at Wayne's little sister. She was sucking her thumb.

"Anyway," Wayne went on, "a pebble's no good for football."

Pip noticed Wayne had on proper football strip and new boots. He cheered up. "Let's play soccer, shall we?"

They went into the park, Cassie trotting between them, still sucking her thumb. Pip eyed her. She was very small. Altogether *too* small to play soccer. What would they do with her?

Wayne had fished out the pebble and was throwing it up into the air. Each time he caught it he shouted, "Yeah, yeah!"

"Have you got a football?" Pip asked, giving him a nudge.

"Watch it!" Wayne clutched at the pebble and missed.

They both made a dive, wrestling about and getting covered with grass and old leaves. Pip still had his haversack on his back, which didn't help. The straps slid down his arms and got in the way. Wriggling free, he made a grab at Wayne's fist and got a handful of dandelion leaves.

Wayne rolled away.

Scrambling up Pip shouted, "Give me my pebble!"

"OK, OK … keep your hair on!" Wayne began to dust himself down. "Anyway, I haven't got your manky pebble!"

"Where is it then?"

"How should I know?"

Pip scowled. "It's got to be somewhere. Give it me!"

"Oh, get lost!" Wayne said, and went marching off towards the sandpit, whistling.

Pip thought of tackling his legs, then noticed Cassie crouched down, gazing at something in her hand.

The pebble!

"That's mine!" He went to take it but Cassie's fat little fingers curled up tight. She shook her head so fiercely Pip wasn't sure what to do. He wanted that pebble badly. But he couldn't fight her. She was too titchy. And Wayne was no use – he was a million kilometres away, by the sandpit, talking to Daniel.

"Oh, bog!" Pip said crossly and picked up his haversack.

"Me see ... me see…" Cassie scratched at the canvas, trying to feel what was inside. She had a funny little voice that made him think of his bear before her squeak wore out.

"Nothing to see." Pip crossed his fingers to cancel the fib, then tried to hitch the haversack out of reach. "Come on, Cassie – let's go!"

To his surprise she got up and trundled along beside him, still clutching the pebble. But she hadn't given up. He could feel her patting the bulge that was Brenda, talking in breathy little hiccups:

"Want to see … in there … me see!"

Pip began to walk more quickly. He could hear Wayne and Daniel arguing about something. Beyond them, a boy he didn't know was doing clever things with his feet and a football. A tall girl was hanging about, watching.

"Hey, Pip!" Daniel thumbed towards the soccer star. "Go on, ask him."

Pip knew what Daniel meant but pretended not to. "Ask what?"

"If he'll play soccer with us, of course!"

Pip shrugged off the haversack in a casual sort of way while he thought about this.

"OK, I'll ask," Wayne said, as if he had meant to all along. He strolled over to the soccer star, giving the football a little nudge with his boot.

Pip wished now he'd done the asking. But

suddenly the ball was heading his way! Not hard and straight, but mincing here and there as if attached by a piece of elastic to the soccer star's boots. He took a deep breath and jigged about, getting ready to kick.

But at the very last minute Wayne bounded between. "Kevin says yes if we play the Cup Final," he was bawling, as if the rest of them were at the other end of the park.

"Right." Daniel became very busy, shoving Pip's haversack into position with his toe. Peeling off his own sweater. Dumping it on the grass a little way off. "Goalposts. We'll need sticks for the other end."

Pip let Daniel and the others rush about. Sticks seemed to be scarce. While he was waiting he looked to see if Cassie might have finished with the pebble and dropped it. She was squatting down picking daisies. The pebble was on the ground, tucked between her feet. He strolled towards her, meaning to say, "You don't want that, do you?" But Daniel came galloping up.

"They're ready – come on!"

Pip edged temptingly close to the football. He took another deep breath, squeezed up his eyes and was just about to give the ball a massive kick when –

"Hang on!" Daniel bellowed. "We haven't fixed the teams yet! This is how it will be: Kevin and me are the home team. You two can be the visitors. I'm captain."

Opening his eyes, Pip saw the soccer star's round face turn so red the freckles on his nose stood out like mud splashes.

"*I'm* captain!" Kevin said loudly. "It's *my* ball. And you can't have a home team in the

Cup Final. There aren't any at Wembley."

"Well, you can't have two captains in one team," Daniel said firmly.

Kevin scowled. "I never said two. Just one. *Me!*"

"Knickers! I am."

"Oh, shut up, Dan!" Wayne was dancing about, doing warm-up exercises.

Daniel stuck his chin in the air and, putting two fingers in his mouth, let out a piercing whistle, trying to kick the ball at the same time.

But Kevin was already halfway to the far goal, the ball running ahead of him.

Daniel bawled, "Foul … foul… You didn't wait… I wasn't ready…"

"You aren't ref!" Kevin shouted. "It's my ball so I'm captain."

"You should've waited!"

"Who says?"

"It's rules!"

"Stuff off!"

"Cheat!"

A real shouting match. Nobody listening. Everyone yelling at the top of their voices. Pip didn't join in. Instead, he looked for the ball.

Somehow it had run away from Kevin and come to rest quite near the tall girl. Pip watched her nip forward and kick – hard and straight.

The ball flew neatly between the two little heaps of sticks.

"Goal ... goal!" She waved her hands above her head.

The shouting stopped. Everybody stared. The girl grinned.

She looked a bit like a stork, Pip thought. Long and thin with a beaky nose and a lot of feathery hair. Secretly he was rather pleased by the way she had shut everyone up.

The girl stuffed her hands in the pockets of her jeans and rocked on her heels, staring at the football team in a cocky sort of way.

"It's a draw," Pip said quickly before the row could start again.

After a second Daniel nodded. "Yes. A draw."

But Kevin said, "No, it isn't. It's half-time. We should have drinks and bits of orange to suck."

Quickly, Pip brought the tube of Fizzers out of his pocket, and handed them round.

"Now..." Kevin licked the froth off his lips. "I'll be captain of Coventry City."

Pip saw Daniel open his mouth and knew if he didn't do something fast the arguments would start again.

"You be captain of the other side, Dan," he suggested. "It's Manchester United." He knew Daniel's dad came from Manchester.

"Oh," said Daniel.

Pip held his breath.

"OK!" Daniel's fingers went to his mouth. Another shrieking whistle ... and he and Kevin both kicked.

This time the ball rose high into the air. They watched it sail away, and bounce down just in front of a pair of scuffed trainers.

As if she had been expecting it, the stork-girl began to dribble the ball up the pitch, heading for the haversack-sweater goalposts. Past Kevin, past Daniel, past Wayne.

Pip was so amazed he forgot to be in the game. Several things seemed to happen all at the same time. He saw Cassie this side of the goalpost pulling Brenda out of his haversack. Then the stork-girl's foot swung back. Next, a great THWACK! and there was Cassie rolling backwards, something clutched in her fat little arms.

Bear or ball? He couldn't see. He ran.

So did everyone else.

The stork-girl got there first. "Did I hurt you?" She crouched down by Cassie.

They lay in a heap. Cassie and Brenda with the ball sandwiched between.

Pip didn't quite know what to do, especially when Cassie let go of the ball but hung on to the bear.

"Saved by your old ted!" Daniel picked up the football and bounced it on Brenda's head. To Pip's relief he didn't ask why she wasn't still where they'd buried her in the mud patch in Pip's back garden. Instead, he burst out laughing.

"Freaky luck," Kevin said admiringly. "What's its name?"

"Just Bear!" Daniel said, saving Pip from having to give away the secret name.

Grabbing the bear's single ear, Daniel pulled.

Cassie hung on.

"Don't," said the stork-girl. "It might come off."

Pip was pleased that she minded.

Daniel stopped pulling but didn't let go. "Just Bear can be our mascot. All top teams have mascots."

"It's a bit manky for a mascot," Wayne objected.

"So what!" the stork-girl said. "Shows it's been lucky for a long time."

Pip began to like her. She helped Cassie up – Cassie still hanging on to Brenda – and there in the grass underneath was his pebble! He picked it up and turned it over, looking at the little brown root lines. Suddenly he held it out.

"Swap?"

Cassie clutched the bear more tightly. She stared at the pebble, then at Pip, then back at Brenda. Slowly a big grin spread across her face. Grabbing the pebble, she handed over the mascot.

Pip heaved a sigh of relief. "Anyone want another Fizzer?" he asked.

There were just enough to go round.

Pip and Daniel spent some time drawing.

The Log Cabin

"Can I have this?" Pip held up a leftover roll of wallpaper.

Mum looked down from the top of the stepladder. "Which?"

"This!" he pushed it under her nose.

"Oh, that! All right. Now do get from under my feet." She began pasting again and a spot of glue flipped off her brush and landed on Pip's ear.

Pip wiped it away. Not fair, he thought crossly. It was the *steps* that were under her feet!

"I'm going to see Daniel, OK?" Without giving her time to say it wasn't, he nipped out of the front door. The wallpaper went with him, and his haversack. It always did.

Daniel lived round the corner in a brick house with a picture of a dog's head on the gate above a notice that said:

BE CAREFUL – I LIVE HERE

The first time Pip had gone to Daniel's house, he'd asked, "Where's the dog?"

"We haven't got one," Daniel had said.

"Then what's that notice for?"

"Just in case we do."

"A puppy would be great!" Pip had imagined it racing about.

"We could take it for walks."

At the time, Daniel was collecting bits of wood and didn't answer.

Pip stared at the growing pile. "What are those sticks for?"

"The Log Cabin, of course," Daniel had

said, as if expecting Pip to know. "I shall live in it for ever and ever. You can live there too if you like."

Pip had been thrilled.

He felt the same shivery sort of thrill today as he opened Daniel's gate. The dog's head picture was still there. Looking at it he had a Wonderful Idea.

He went up the path.

Daniel opened the front door. "What's that for?" He grabbed at the wallpaper.

Pip hung on. "Our Log Cabin."

"Paper on the walls?" Daniel scoffed. "Everybody knows Log Cabins are all wood!"

"Paper for drawing plans on!" Pip pulled the wallpaper away. "There's masses. Enough for a hundred blueprints." He could tell that Daniel didn't know what a blueprint was. "Let's unroll a bit, so we can draw some of the rooms and where the windows and doors go. Like my grandad did for his new garage." And in case Daniel was still in a muddle, he added, "That's what blueprints are – building plans."

"The paper's white, not blue." Daniel led the way into the kitchen.

"Doesn't matter." Pip began to spread the wallpaper over the table. "Have you got Biros and felt-tips and things?"

They spent some time drawing the shapes of the rooms. Then more time arguing what was to go in them.

"We'll need sleeping bags and straw to make beds and mugs and tools and a camping stove…"

"They won't let us have that," Pip said. "In case it tips over and burns things."

Daniel screwed up his face. "Well, sticks for a camp-fire then, and matches and a saucepan and chocolate cake and fudge…"

Daniel's dad came in at this point and said it was much too nice to stay indoors and to hop it.

Picking up their blueprint, they took it into the garden.

A strong breeze was blowing and they had to kneel on the end of the paper to stop it flapping.

Pip remembered his wonderful idea. "We shall need a guard dog." He slid a sideways look at Daniel and saw the tip of Daniel's tongue sticking out between his teeth. He was drawing a careful window.

"What for?" Daniel asked when he'd finished.

"To guard our Log Cabin when we aren't there." Pip put a kennel underneath the window.

Daniel began to stir round and round with

his black felt-tip as if it was a wooden spoon. "I told you, we haven't got a dog."

"Why don't you ask your dad for one?" Pip suggested. "My mum says our house is too small… But you've got a notice on your gate already." He watched the dark scribble get bigger and bigger. "What's that?"

"A bed for Just Bear."

Pip was startled. Secretly he had imagined Brenda sharing the Log Cabin, but hadn't liked to mention it. "That doesn't look much like a bed," he said doubtfully, and thought of his bear comfortably curled up in the bottom of his haversack with a woolly scarf wrapped round her thin legs.

Daniel spotted the kennel. "Look – the bed can go in there. A guard bear – lots fiercer than a guard dog!" and he laughed so much he dropped his felt-tip.

Pip didn't think this at all funny. He gave

the kennel a door and put a padlock on it.

Just then the strong breeze turned into a bad-tempered wind, whooshing the blue-print into some cabbages.

As Pip chased it, Daniel's face brightened. "I know – why don't we go and hunt for a place to build our Log Cabin? Better than drawing soppy plans."

Pip looked vaguely round Daniel's garden.

"Not here. Full up," Daniel said.

The garden did seem to be packed tight with vegetables. Pip thought of his own garden which was even smaller.

"There's lots of room in the empty house garden," he said slowly.

Daniel beamed. "Stay here while I get some food."

Pip watched him rush indoors and wondered why Daniel always needed to eat before he did anything. He fidgeted about, and had just stowed the wallpaper in the shed when Daniel hurtled back into the garden dressed in his army camouflage outfit, dragging his kit bag behind him.

"I've got chocolate biscuits and coconut biscuits and Jammy Dodgers ... lots and lots so we won't starve."

Pip thought this unlikely as they were only going to the end of Daniel's street, where the empty house stood on the corner.

The empty house was a great place. Once he had sneaked through the front gate with Daniel and Wayne for a look through the dirty windows. Another time they had gone in the back way, squeezing through a broken bit of fence where the garden bumped up against the park. They had made a tunnel through some wild bushes, and played space aliens.

Today they chose the back way, scrambling through the fence and pushing into the tunnel again. The sun had gone behind a cloud and the bushes seemed very tall and dark. They were full of prickles too, and the wind was making a funny moaning sound. Perhaps the empty house wasn't such a good idea after all.

A nettle stung Pip's cheek.

"Ow!" He stopped crawling and dumped his haversack. "Why don't we try somewhere else?"

"What's the matter – scared we'll get caught?" Daniel asked in the sort of way that made Pip say hurriedly, " 'Course not. Nobody lives here. I think it's too messy for building our Log Cabin, that's all."

But Daniel was already barging ahead. "Come on!"

Pip stayed where he was. "Dan … listen!"

But Daniel was making far too much noise

scrabbling over dead leaves and sticks to bother with anything else.

Pip listened harder. There it was again! A sort of scuffling noise. Prickly feelings began to walk down the back of his neck. Daniel didn't know about the Whatever-It-Was. Pip didn't want him to get a fright. Diving after Daniel's legs, he bumped his nose, on the kit bag ... and remembered too late he had left his haversack behind. He was about to turn back when the Whatever-It-Was happened again.

Crashing noises this time…

"Listen!" Daniel hissed.

Pip began to say, "I was trying to tell you…" when Daniel whispered fiercely:

"Shut up! *Listen!*"

As the crashing got louder, Pip thought – something HUGE! He imagined lots of very sharp teeth. Then there was no more time for thinking. With a final *CRASH*, the Whatever-It-Was bounced out of the bushes and straight on top of him. A wet tongue slapped him across the eye.

"Get off!" Pip rolled over … and saw that the something HUGE was nothing more than a little squirming puppy.

A voice yelled, "Come here … bad dog … come *here*!"

More crashing. Then, "Oh!" and a surprised, "Hi!"

Pip pushed the puppy away and, scrambling out of the tunnel, saw the stork-girl who had been on the park and had kicked that great goal. She was face to face with Daniel.

"What are you doing here?" She was frowning.

Daniel shoved his hands in his pockets. "What's it to do with you?" he said rudely.

"I live here."

Pip and Daniel looked at the girl, then at each other.

Pip recovered first. "But the house is empty!"

"Not any more." She tried to pick up the puppy but it got away. "We're moving in right now. The furniture van's just come. Mum told me to keep that holy terror out of the way, so we came out here... Oh stink, where's he gone now?"

She seemed to have forgotten about why they were in her back garden. Pip felt relieved the Log Cabin was still a secret.

"Does he come if you whistle?" Daniel stuck his fingers in his mouth and tried.

Pip didn't wait for results. He was thinking about something else. He began wriggling back along the tunnel.

The puppy was there, just as Pip had been

afraid it would be. Its fat little black rump stuck out from the haversack. Muffled growls came from inside. Pip grabbed its back legs and pulled. Still growling, the rest of the puppy appeared, dragging Brenda by one arm.

Before Pip could decide what to do, the stork-girl was there.

"Let go, you terror!" She scooped up the puppy.

But the terror didn't want to let go. Brenda dangled forlornly by her skinny arm. Suddenly this was too much, and Pip gave the puppy a sharp tap across its nose.

A little yelp, and Brenda fell to the ground.

"You shouldn't hit him!" the girl said indignantly. "He isn't your dog. Serve you right if he bit you. Bet he will!" She put the puppy on the ground.

The puppy didn't want to let go.

Surprised but not sorry, Pip rescued Brenda, all the time keeping a wary eye on the holy terror. But instead of trying to bite him, the puppy romped around making little dashes at Pip's trainers, worrying the laces, then jumped up to lick his hand.

The girl looked disgusted. "You'll never make a guard dog."

Pip decided to test this. With Brenda safely under his arm he knelt down. "Good dog," he said. "Sit!"

The holy terror didn't seem to understand. Instead he leapt on to Pip's knees and sat panting.

"He likes you," Daniel said.

"Good Gee Dee," Pip stroked him.

"What's a G. D.?" the girl asked.

"Short for Guard Dog." Pip eased Brenda from under the puppy's paw. "Has he got a name?"

"My dad calls him Stinker, but I like Gee Dee better."

"What does your dad call you?" Pip looked at her expectantly.

"Judith."

He felt a tiny bit disappointed. He'd hoped for Storky or even Mop, with hair like that. "I'm Pip."

"I'm Daniel Higgs," Daniel said. "And we need a guard dog for the Log Cabin. We said so, didn't we, Pip?"

Pip remembered it rather differently, but nodded. He was amazed that Daniel had let out their secret. Not that he minded now. He tried a soft little whistle.

Gee Dee's ears twitched and his tail thumped. Pip wasn't sure if he was being obedient or just nosy, but training a guard dog had to start somewhere. Pulling Daniel's kit bag closer, he fished out some biscuits and gave one to Gee Dee.

"Good dog!" he said.

Gee Dee gobbled it down and slithered off Pip's knees, ready to finish the rest. Pip shoved them back.

Gee Dee cocked his head on one side hopefully.

Pip glanced at Judith to see if more biscuits were all right, but she and Daniel were busy arguing about how to build the log cabin in a tree.

"Just one more then!" He took out another biscuit. "Shake a paw." He held out his hand.

Gee Dee licked it.

It was more of a wash than a handshake, but it was a good start. Pip gave him the biscuit.

"High time you cleared out some of your old toys."

Pip's Tip

"This place is a tip!" Mum stood in the doorway of Pip's bedroom and looked around.

Pip looked too. It seemed all right to him.

"High time you cleared out some of your old toys," she went on.

"Why?" Pip liked his toys.

"Because there's hardly room to move. With Christmas not far off, if you don't get rid of some of *this*," dabbing with her finger, "there won't be any space for your new presents."

He hadn't thought of that.

"I'll find you some plastic bags. See how

many you can fill," she said.

"What will you do with them?" Pip asked nervously.

But Mum was already halfway down the stairs and didn't hear.

Pip walked back into his room. What was he going to throw out?

Maybe his box of old bricks?

He tipped them on to the floor and built a wall. Just the sort of wall he needed for keeping in his farm animals.

He left the bricks and rummaged through the bag of sticks he'd collected for the log cabin. Most were too thin, and anyway the log cabin had turned into a sort of tree tent in Judith's garden. But sticks were handy for all sorts of things. Like stirring his pots of experiments. Or to throw for Gee Dee to fetch.

He made up his mind to hunt out broken

things instead, and the squashy baby toys he'd grown out of...

He looked at Brenda.

Brenda looked back at him – or one eye did. The other stared sadly down at her saggy middle and thin legs.

She'd been with him all his life. Since he was born.

Definitely a baby toy, though nobody could say she was squashy.

Too much of her insides had fallen out. A *very* old worn bear... But she wasn't just any old bear. She was something else now, something very important – their team mascot! How could he throw that out?

As he pulled her from the shelf for a closer inspection, a heap of comics, a broken tennis racquet and several boxes came too. Paper and jigsaw pieces spread around his feet.

But Pip didn't give them a second glance. He was staring in delight at his water-bottle and the baseball cap he'd spent ages trying to find. All this time they'd been hiding behind the comics!

Dropping Brenda, he grabbed the cap, put it on with the peak sticking out at one side. Then dashed into the bathroom to fill his water-bottle. A quick swig...

"Yuck! Mushrooms!"

"PIP!"

Pip jumped. He rushed back to his room. Mum was pointing to the muddle of jigsaws and comics.

"That's not sorting out. That's making a worse mess!"

"I have to look behind things, you know," Pip explained. "If I don't, how can I sort them out?"

Mum gave him a funny look, and dumped

some plastic bags on the end of his bed. "Lunch in half an hour. I'll expect a nice tidy room by then." She went downstairs.

Finding his lost cap and water-bottle had given Pip an idea. So many things had gone missing. There was plenty of time to hunt about.

Starting with the underneath shelf, he began to pull everything on to the floor. Mostly broken cardboard boxes with half the games missing. Not much of interest. He moved on to the old tin trunk that had once belonged to Grandad. On top there was a jumble of socks, pants and T-shirts mixed up with his schoolbag and a dipper truck. He swept the lot on to the floor and lifted the lid.

The trunk was brim full. He began digging about. Chucking things out – a jack-in-the-box, plastic ducks, his Action Man with an arm missing, torn scrap-book...

"Wow!" Pip pulled out his gorilla mask and put it on. The baseball cap didn't fit on top, but his cowboy hat did.

Where was his holster?

More things were heaved on to the floor.

There it was! He buckled it round his middle. Now for his guns!

But the guns weren't to be found, though he pulled out drawers, searched in his wardrobe, dragged everything from under his bed.

Junk piled up around him.

Still no guns.

Pip paused for a think. Had he lent them to Daniel? Or Wayne...

"I'll be up in a tick to see how you've got on," Mum called from the bottom of the stairs.

Daniel, that's who, Pip remembered ...

and saw the state of his room.

Up in a tick, Mum had said!

Pip had never worked so fast. Bunging things under the bed. Hurling stuff under his pillow and duvet. Stuffing drawers, the Grandad trunk, his wardrobe. Sweeping the leftovers behind his chair. At the last moment he remembered to shovel a few things into the plastic bags.

Looking through the eye-slits in his gorilla mask he hoped Mum wouldn't notice that the drawers didn't shut properly, nor the trunk lid, even when he sat on it.

"It's a start," she said as she came in. "I see you've decided to throw out your old teddy."

Pip looked at the shelf where Brenda should have been and wasn't. Where had he put her?

Mum gathered up the plastic bags. "Well done, Gorilla! We'll sort them out this afternoon and see if there's anything worth passing on."

Pip felt relieved, then a little bit ashamed, then alarmed. He didn't know what he'd put in those bags. There might be something important. Suppose Brenda had sneaked in? Sometimes she turned up in the most unexpected places.

"Thanks for putting your clean clothes away," Mum said.

What clean clothes? Pip wondered. He followed her slowly downstairs, trying to picture where Brenda had gone.

In the kitchen Mum said, "Where's my boy? I don't think macaroni cheese is the right food for gorillas."

Pip loved macaroni cheese. He took off his cowboy hat and the gorilla mask, deciding to have a proper hunt for Brenda after his second helping.

But after lunch Judith and Wayne called round. Cassie was with them. So was Gee Dee.

Pip ran into the kitchen, Gee Dee bounding in front. "Mum, Wayne and Judith want me to go round to her house … can I?" He didn't like to mention they meant to play in the log-cabin-tent. It was still a sort of secret.

The plastic bags were on the floor and Gee Dee made a dive, knocking one over. Toys and comics slithered out. Gee Dee slithered in.

Mum didn't give Pip a proper answer. "Who's this?"

"Gee Dee," Pip said. He could hear Judith shouting, "Here, boy… *Here!*"

Gee Dee took no notice. Something inside the bag was very interesting. Pip went to look, hoping that it might be Brenda, but it was only an old ball that had lost its bounce.

The others had drifted in and stood in the kitchen doorway.

"Come out of there!" Mum gathered up Gee Dee and gave him a cuddle. "Hello, you three. Pip's been having a turn out." She smiled at Cassie. "Do you like teddy bears?"

Cassie nodded.

"See what you can find in those bags then. Go on – and you two," nodding at Judith and Wayne. Gee Dee was slapping her face with his smooth tongue. She put him down. "Take whatever you like, that's right, isn't it, Pip?"

Pip couldn't think of anything to say. He watched Gee Dee drag out an old sock and shake it hard. Cassie, Wayne and Judith began to rootle through the bags. But when everything had been taken out and put back again, there was still no Brenda. Wayne helped himself to a whistle. Judith took the ball for Gee Dee.

Cassie's face puckered up. "No teddy!"

Mum looked surprised. "Perhaps it fell out. Have a look upstairs. Go with her, Pip."

They all went. Gee Dee was the first to reach Pip's bedroom. He disappeared under the bed.

Wayne said, "Did your mum mean our mascot?"

Pip nodded.

Judith was shocked. "You can't get rid of our mascot!"

Wayne nodded. "Mega bad luck!" He looked at the shelf where Brenda usually sat. "What have you done with it?"

Pip explained about the swift tidy up. "I don't know where I put *anything*," he finished.

"That's no good," Judith said. "Next

weekend Kevin's cousins are coming to stay. He says they're ace at soccer."

Gee Dee was making soft growling noises under the bed.

"We'll need our mascot if we're to beat them," Wayne added. "Come on, Pip, shake your brains. You must know where it is."

"I don't," Pip said crossly. He was fed up with this tidying business. He wished he was in the log-cabin-tent.

The growls got louder and Cassie crouched down, then began to wriggle under the bed.

"You'll have to start looking then, won't you?" Judith opened the Grandad trunk. And closed it again, rather quickly.

"Any luck?" Mum called.

Pip could hear her feet coming up the stairs. He stared helplessly around his bed-room and shook his head as she peered in.

Under the bed Cassie sneezed. Gee Dee began to bark.

"I think someone has sharper eyes than the rest of you!"

Pip looked where Mum was looking, and saw Cassie slithering backwards from under his bed. Feet in blue boots. Red woolly legs. Yellow sweater. Dark curly head.

More growls and barks.

Cassie's squeaky voice said, "Bad dog!"

Scuffling noises and a little yelp from Gee Dee.

Cassie turned over and sat up … *hugging Brenda!* Gee Dee crawled out and began to run in little circles after his own tail. All of them were covered with bits of fluff.

"Fancy that teddy rolling under there." Mum gave Pip another of her funny looks. "Well – finder's keepers. Right, Pip?"

"No!" Pip said desperately. "Not exactly.

I mean…" He looked at Brenda. How could he possibly give her away? But Cassie was staring up at him with a hopeful look in her eyes.

Pip thought fast. "What about a holiday?" As soon as he said it, he felt pleased. Wayne would make sure Brenda's holiday didn't last too long. She had mascot work to do. "You can take the teddy home just for a holiday. OK, Cass?"

" 'Kay!" A big smile spread across Cassie's face. She squeezed Brenda tight against her yellow sweater.

"I can go to Judith's house, can't I, Mum?" Now that Brenda was safe Pip thought he deserved a treat. "I'll finish any tidying tomorrow."

Mum folded her arms and put her head on one side. "Promise?"

"Promise, promise, promise!"

Before Mum could change her mind, Pip was down the stairs stuffing his feet into wellingtons, grabbing his jacket and had dashed out of the front door, Gee Dee at his heels.

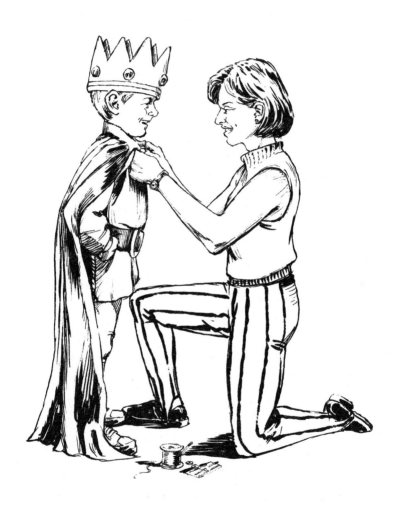

Mum helped Pip make a crown and a red cloak.

THE NATIVITY PLAY

Brenda was having a long holiday. Much too long, Pip thought. Her special place on the shelf in his bedroom looked very empty. He kept meaning to remind Wayne to tell Cassie to give her back. But each time he thought of this, something else got in the way and he forgot. Just now there were so many things waiting to happen...

Like Christmas.

And the end-of-term school party.

Most of all, the Nativity Play.

Ms Crabbe had chosen Pip to be one of the Three Kings, with *Words* to say. Mum helped him make a crown out of cardboard and silver cooking foil, and a red cloak with silver stars up the front. He had a golden box to carry. Pip had helped eat the chocolates a long time ago. But he didn't want the box to stay empty, so he put in a toy motorbike. After all it was Jesus' birthday. Everybody had presents on their birthdays.

Wayne's eyes opened wide when he called round and saw Pip dressed up. "You look like Superman!"

"Can't fly," Pip said, wishing he could. "What colour's your cloak?"

"Purple and it's not a cloak it's my dressing gown. Look!"

Wayne pulled it out of his haversack. "Me and Cassie put the gold spray on."

Pip was impressed. He stroked his finger down one of the gold splashes. "Doesn't your mum mind?"

"She doesn't know. I made Cassie

promise not to tell."

Talking of Cassie reminded Pip of Brenda. "Tell Cassie I want our mascot back, will you?" He chose "mascot" instead of "bear" because it sounded more important.

"OK." Wayne stuffed his dressing gown into his haversack.

The day before the Nativity Play, the Three Kings were in the school playground with Joseph and Mary. The third King (Kevin) moaned about all the Words he was supposed to learn.

"You should know them by now," Pip said, and gabbled, " 'Where-is-the-baby-show-us-the-way!' See – it's easy!"

"Those aren't my Words." Kevin put on his yellow cloak.

"What do you have to say then?" Pip asked.

"Can't remember." Kevin plonked the crown made of wire and shiny green bottle tops on his head.

Daniel suggested, "Why don't you write your Words on your hand in Biro? That's what I'm going to do." He was being Joseph and had quite a lot to say.

Secretly Pip thought this a good idea and decided to do the same. Not that he would need to look. He knew his Words back to front.

"I shan't forget *my* Words," Hyacinth said smugly. She was being Mary, Jesus' mother.

Jesus didn't have Words. He was too small to talk. In fact, he wasn't real. Hyacinth was bringing her special doll to be a pretend Baby Jesus. It could cry and wet its nappy.

"You have to pour water into its mouth first," Hyacinth told them.

Walking to school on Nativity Play Day, Pip wondered if Jesus had cried and wet his nappy. All babies did. But what if Jesus was different? Pip thought he would ask his teacher. Ms Crabbe knew everything. Well, almost. She wasn't too good at football-match results.

Under his breath he muttered, " 'Where is the baby? Show us the way. Where is the baby…' " every now and again checking the Biro Words on his hand to make sure he said them right. Secretly he thought Baby Jesus was lucky not to have Words.

Much later, in the classroom, he remembered his question and waved his hand in the air.

Ms Crabbe made a tutting noise. "It's almost dinner-time, Pip. Can't you wait…?"

Pip was about to explain he didn't want to go to the toilet, when he noticed

Hyacinth scrabbling about inside her bag in a worried sort of way. He put his hand down and watched.

Ms Crabbe clapped for silence. "I hope everyone has remembered their costume?"

Everyone nodded – except Hyacinth, Pip saw, almost forgetting to nod himself.

"Right! Get into groups, please." Ms Crabbe pointed at the table near her desk. "Three Kings over here. Shepherds by the door. Mary and Joseph by the nature table. Donkey and Calf, come and stand by the cupboard. Angel Gabriel..." She glanced round the classroom. "Anyone know where Judith is?"

"Please, Mizz, Hyacinth said Judith forgot her wings and went back home for them after break," Wayne said.

Hyacinth turned bright pink. "I never! I said she said..."

"Yes, you did," Wayne interrupted.

"Didn't!"

"Did! And you said you'd forgotten … ow!" Wayne hopped about. "Hyacinth trod on me, Mizz!"

"Your foot got in the way!" Hyacinth glared as if she was ready to tread on his other foot.

Pip could see she was in a bit of a stew. He was about to ask Wayne what it was all about, when Ms Crabbe said sharply, "That's enough, you two!"

Just then the door opened and Judith rushed in, hot and bothered.

"I left my wings in our kitchen, Mizz. I thought I'd have to go back for them. I told Hyacinth I was going, but then it was all right because my mum found them. She brought them to school for me." Judith held up a carrier bag.

"You'll forget your head one of these days, Judith," Ms Crabbe said, raising her eyebrows.

Everyone laughed.

Pip was glad he hadn't forgotten anything. He did a quick check on the golden box to make sure the motorbike was still inside.

It was.

Soon afterwards the bell sounded and they all rushed off to have their dinners.

When he had eaten his sandwiches and yogurt, Pip went into the playground and kicked a football around with Kevin. The game was fast and exciting, and the dinner hour was almost over before Pip noticed Daniel and Wayne talking in an urgent sort of a way with Judith and Hyacinth. He knew it must be important or they would have joined in the game.

He went over to them. "Hi! What's up?"

"No Baby Jesus," Daniel told him.

Pip thought he was joking. "Ha-ha!"

Daniel looked at Hyacinth. "Go on, you tell him."

"I had too much to carry this morning," she said in a wobbly voice. "So I left my doll at home."

"That's not what you told me," Wayne said. "You told me you forgot."

Hyacinth glowered at him, then gave a hiccupy sob. "I g-go home for dinner. Coming back was when I f-forgot. I left Baby Jesus on the b-bus."

This was a stunner.

They stared at each other.

"Does Mizz know?" Pip asked.

Hyacinth shook her head. "She'll kill me!"

Most of the time Pip thought Hyacinth was a pain, but now he felt sorry for her. She looked so miserable. "No, she won't," he said quickly. "We'll think of something."

"Like what?" Judith asked.

Pip's middle had a sudden empty feeling. Any minute now the bell would go. In no time the nativity play would begin. He glanced desperately round the playground. Then out through the railings. Already a few mums and dads were there, chatting as they waited to come in. Some grandmas and grandpas too. He saw his own granny in her best coat with a new big red and blue scarf round her neck. She was talking to Wayne's mum, who was holding Cassie's hand.

Daniel folded his arms. "Go on then! Suggest something."

They were all waiting. Judith rocking on her heels. Wayne and Kevin grinning. Hyacinth looking as if she expected him to do some magic trick.

"We could roll up a sweater," Pip said feebly. "A pretend baby doll. No one would know."

"Oh yes, and what do we wrap it in? A tea towel?" Judith was very scornful.

Just then the bell sounded.

Lining up with the others, Pip turned to ask Wayne if he had any bright ideas, but couldn't see him. Before he could think about this, Ms Crabbe, who was on playground duty, put a hand on his shoulder.

"Take my mug back to the dining-room for me, Pip. Give it to one of the dinner ladies ... and *don't run*!"

Pip took the mug, sneaking a sideways look to see if she seemed bothered. She didn't. But surely she must have noticed that Baby Jesus was missing? He imagined the fuss when she did find out. He felt glad he wasn't Hyacinth, and dawdled back to the classroom not looking forward to the trouble. But when he got there everyone was busy changing into their costumes and all Ms Crabbe said was, "You took your time, Pip. Hurry up and get changed."

Pip darted a look round the classroom. A buzz of excited conversation. Somebody giggled. But no trouble! He couldn't understand it.

Taking off his sweater he rolled it up. With some sort of shawl thing it might pass as Baby Jesus. Not such a bad idea after all.

"How about this?" he said to Kevin.

But Kevin was on hands and knees hunting for one of the bottle tops that had fallen off his crown. "Mind your feet," was all he said.

Pip put on his cloak. Wayne was still nowhere to be seen.

Perhaps he wasn't feeling well. Perhaps he had gone to the sick room. That meant only two Kings were left.

"Where's Wayne?" he asked Judith as she poked her head out of her long white Angel nightie. But before she could answer, Ms Crabbe came to tie on the golden Angel wings.

"Out of the way, Pip," she said.

Pip retreated to the cupboard, where the Donkey and Calf were already dressed. But it was no good asking them because they couldn't hear with their heads on.

Pip felt worried. No Baby Jesus and now no Wayne! Things were getting worse and worse.

But just as he thought this Wayne came in slamming the door.

"Quietly!" Ms Crabbe said. "Everything all right, Wayne?"

Pip saw Wayne nod and wanted to ask what was happening, but didn't get a chance.

"Line up, everyone," Ms Crabbe said. "Time to go down to the hall. Don't push, Hyacinth! No rushing any of you … and no shouting either. Good Luck!"

All the curtains in the school hall were drawn, except the stage curtains. They were open. Pip walked across to one of the shepherds and said:

"Show us the way. Where is the baby?"

As soon as the Words fell out, he knew he'd said them back to front. He heard Kevin snigger. Had anyone else noticed? He sneaked a look at the people who had come to see the nativity play. There was his granny, smiling as she saw him look at her.

Nobody laughed. Pip felt better. Until he remembered about Baby Jesus.

"The shepherds say the baby is in the stable," Kevin read off his hand, as he tramped noisily across the stage in his football boots. He bumped into Pip, shoving him into Wayne.

"Watch it!" Wayne hissed, pushing his crown out of his eyes.

Hyacinth and Daniel were sitting on classroom chairs in the middle of a lot of straw with the Donkey and Calf close by. Wayne marched over to them.

"We have brought presents." He fished in one pocket after another. "Sorry … can't find mine…"

Pip quickly offered his golden box, though there didn't seem much point now Baby Jesus was missing.

"What is He called?" he asked – because

*The scarf was wrapped round something
that had a baby sort of shape.*

Wayne had forgotten to say this bit.

"The baby's name is Jesus," Hyacinth said.

Daniel took the golden box.

Pip hoped that Daniel wouldn't think the motorbike was for him. He saw that Hyacinth was nursing some kind of bundle. Saw his granny's red and blue scarf wrapped round something that had a baby sort of shape…

No, it couldn't be…

He blinked and stared again to make sure there was no mistake…

BRENDA!

Not much of her showed. Just the tip of her black nose and two furry feet sticking out at the bottom of the shawl-scarf.

Hyacinth was cuddling her just as if she was a real baby.

The Donkey made a hee-hawing noise and the Calf mooed.

Pip felt like cheering.

But how had Brenda come to be in school? Pip squeezed up his eyes trying to think … and remembered Cassie waiting outside the railings. She must have brought Brenda with her and Wayne knew and…

Suddenly Pip realized nobody had said Words for rather a long time. He nudged Daniel.

"We-are-in-the-stable-because-there-was-no-room-in-the-Inn," Daniel gabbled.

Judith raised her arms making the golden Angel wings shake.

Ms Crabbe began to play "Away in a Manger" on the piano, nodding to the rest of the class to remind them to sing.

Pip blew out his cheeks with relief. Everything was all right and the Nativity Play was almost over. Tomorrow was the school party. He was looking forward to that! Perhaps there would be sausage rolls. They would be hot and sizzly. His mouth watered as he imagined biting into one ... two ... three...

"Happy Birthday!"

PROPERLY EIGHT

The knocker banged loudly. Pip ran to open the front door. There was Daniel in his Australian hat with the corks dangling round the brim. He had a cricket bat under his arm.

Pip grinned. He liked cricket and needed a new bat.

"Happy Birthday," Daniel said. "You don't look any different from yesterday."

Pip thought being properly eight ought to show. He checked quickly on the bit of himself he could see. Legs. Feet in old trainers. Arms and hands. All much the same. He felt disappointed.

Before he could find out if the bat was his present, Daniel barged past, asking, "What's for tea? I'm hungry."

"Food," Pip said quickly. He didn't want to give away the surprise. "It isn't time for tea yet." He eyed the bat. Close to, it didn't seem very new.

"Can I play with those old cars then?" Daniel didn't wait for an answer. He galloped upstairs, the bat still under his arm.

Pip opened his mouth to tell him about the special party game he'd planned in the garden, when someone called, "Hi, Pip!"

Wayne in a spaceman's suit was coming through the open door, towing Cassie. She was wearing a nurse's uniform and carrying a small pink teddy bear with a bandage over one eye.

"I had to bring her." Wayne let go of Cassie's hand. He glanced at Pip to see if he minded.

Pip did mind. Cassie was too small to play the special birthday game. He was about to say so, when over the top of Cassie's head he caught sight of Superman and, behind him, a White Sheet with eyes peering through cut-out holes.

"Hi, Pip!" Kevin took off the Superman mask.

"Hooo, booo-woo-woo," moaned the White Sheet.

The two followed Wayne and Cassie, who were following Daniel up the stairs.

Pip suddenly realized that for some reason he didn't know about, he was the only one in ordinary clothes.

He bounded after them. "Who said wear dressing-up clothes?"

Nobody answered. He saw Wayne crouched

over *his* Lego garage busy working the crane. And what cheek – Kevin was piling bricks into his *new* birthday pick-up truck! The White Sheet was less of a bother – drifting about practising ghostly howls.

Pip looked for Daniel. The Australian hat lay next to the bat on top of the bed. Muffled racing car noises came from underneath. *"Brm brm ... brm brrrrm..."*

Pip prodded Daniel's foot which was sticking out.

"It's Waldoni in the lead." Daniel's voice sounded as if it were shut in the airing cupboard. "He's taking the bend too fast ... brrrrm ... eeeow ... and Curtis is on his tail, he's catching up... LOOK OUT!"

Ear-bursting thumps and screeches.

"Curtis has crashed! He's on fire... Police ... ambulance..."

The bedroom echoed with siren noises as

Kevin gave the brand-new pick-up truck a tremendous shove, making it crash into the legs of the bed.

"Hey, mind what..." Pip broke off, seeing Cassie reaching for his bear. "NO... DON'T..." He leapt to save the shelf from tipping as it always did, but was too late. A shower of books, comics, felt-tips, football boots, his plasticine owl, two jigsaws and a sock that had stuck to the Mars bar he'd forgotten to finish tumbled on top of her. Pip was amazed there was so much stuff after all the clearing up he'd done.

Cassie didn't seem to mind. She sat in the middle of the mess, hugging the bear. "Brenda!" she said lovingly – and began to eat the Mars bar.

Pip couldn't believe his ears. How could Cassie know this very secret name? He checked on the others. But none of them

Cassie sat in the middle of the mess.

seemed to have heard.

"Cassie's always wrecking things." Wayne was untangling the crane-hook from the pink bear's bandage.

Pip started again. "Listen. How about if…"

More whooping siren noises buried Pip's voice. Kevin wriggled after the truck. The White Sheet went on drifting and making ghostly moans. Pip began to feel a bit ghostly himself. Kneeling down, he peered under the bed.

"Listen, you two," he said. "How about if we…"

A Ferrari racer whizzed past the tip of his nose. Something fell over his feet.

The ghostly moans turned to a shriek.

Next thing, Pip was smothered in folds of cloth. The bed bounced. Struggling up into free air, he saw Judith scowling.

"Now look what you've done!" She slid off the bed, shrugging away the last of the sheet.

"I didn't do anything!" Pip said indignantly.

"Well, it's squashed."

"What is?"

She pulled a crumpled yellow parcel from the pocket of her shorts and said gloomily, "Happy Birthday."

"Oh!" Pip took the parcel. Inside was a flattened box, and inside that, Maltesers. They were a bit crumbly but tasted good. "Thanks," he said, then, "Who said it was a dressing-up party?"

"Kevin did."

Kevin stuck his head out from under the bed. "Here!" A hand appeared clutching a paper bag. "Forgot. Sorry!"

The bag was full of badges.

"Eight – one for each year," Kevin explained.

"Great!" Pip said, adding, "Who told you to dress up?"

"Wayne." Kevin vanished again.

Pip had just finished pinning MICE ARE NICE!, DENNIS THE MENACE! and I'M BATS ABOUT BOOKS! to his T-shirt, when Wayne fished something from inside his space suit.

"Who told you it was a dressing-up party?" Pip asked quickly.

"Cassie did. Happy Birthday Present!"

"Sunglasses!" Pip put them on and looked in his mirror. "Cool!" He turned round to see them from the other side and came face to face with Daniel, the cricket bat in his hand.

Daniel whacked at the air. Bits of under-bed fluff dropped off him. "I've hit a few balls with this. You don't mind, do you?" He passed it to Pip. "You can have the hat as well if you like."

Pip couldn't believe his luck. He stroked the bat. Picked up the wonderful hat. It was a bit squashed since Judith fell on it, but he didn't care. Pushing out the dents, he put it on. Through the darkness of his new sunglasses he could see the corks bobbing about.

"Come on," he said. "Let's go in the garden. We can play cricket. I've put the stumps ready."

Judith cheered up. "Can I bowl first?"

"OK by me!" Wayne abandoned the crane. Kevin and Daniel were already rushing downstairs.

Cassie was nursing the old bear.

"Who told you to dress up?" Pip asked her.

"Nobody." She stared at him as if he was being stupid, then looked down at her uniform. "Brenda's leg's broke. She's in hospital. I'm nurse. I telled everybody to dress up." Cassie was much more chatty these days.

"Oh," Pip said. "Come on."

"Yes, come on, Cass..." Wayne didn't seem to have noticed the name. He jigged about.

Cassie's bottom lip wobbled. "Brenda like cricket. And Grub does!"

"Who's Grub?" Pip asked.

"Her manky pink ted," Wayne said, screwing up his face as if something smelled bad.

Judith held out her hand to Cassie. "Brenda's all right. She's gone to sleep."

Brenda again! Pip shot a surprised look at Judith, but she was behaving as if the name was something she had always known.

Cassie didn't budge. Two tears ran between the smears of chocolate on her cheeks.

This was turning out a funny sort of birthday, Pip thought, crossly. He wondered whether to snatch Brenda and hurl her downstairs? No. Cassie would howl.

He thought fast. Going to his school bag he scrabbled about and pulled out a ruler.

"Look! Here's a crutch to help Brenda walk." Saying the secret name out loud was suddenly easy and a great relief. Pip put the ruler under his own arm, pretending to limp along. "See, like this!"

Cassie took the ruler-crutch and fitted Brenda's thin arm over it. "Carry Grub for Brenda," she said.

"What d'you mean, *for Brenda*?" Pip took hold of the one-eyed pink teddy.

Cassie's two eyes looked at him and her eyebrows came together in a scowl. "I *said*. Her leg's broke. She can't carry – and Grub's her birdee present!"

"All right!" Pip said hastily, trying not to show how amazed he was. How had Cassie known that today was Brenda's birthday as well as his? He was about to ask her, when the wonderful smell of fish and chips drifted up the stairs.

His mouth went all juicy.

Judith had dashed downstairs, and Cassie was already shuffling along on her knees, making Brenda hobble in front. Pip followed, carrying Grub and the bat, and trying to imagine what sort of a birthday cake he would find waiting.

They went into the garden. On the grass was a big plastic cloth with fish and chips still in their wrappings, just as he'd asked.

Cans of lemonade as well, and ...

His eyes opened wide.

"A cricket match!" He'd imagined a hedgehog cake, or an engine cake, or even a pick-up truck cake, but this was the best ever!

There were tiny cricketers standing on the green icing, with bats and stumps and a red mini ball. Written in curly white icing round the edge were the words: "EIGHT TODAY – HAPPY BIRTHDAY, PIP – EIGHT TODAY!"

He took off his sunglasses to make sure there was no mistake and saw the colours brighten. "W-o-w!"

"Can we start?" Daniel rubbed his middle. "I'm starving."

"Brenda's hungry, too," Cassie said.

Pip decided that both cricket matches would have to wait.

He began to dole out the bundles of fish

and chips, squatting down when he got to Cassie. Very quietly he asked, "How did you know the teddy's name was Brenda?"

Cassie ate a chip. Then another. "Brenda told me," she said.

Pip knew this couldn't be true. Teddy bears were only toys, and toys couldn't speak. But he gave Brenda a careful look and thought he saw her glass eyes twinkle.

Sunlight, he decided firmly. Twinkles of sunlight. Must be! All the same, it didn't seem like any old twinkle.

Keeping a watchful eye on Brenda, he began to eat his birthday chips.

THE

END